P9-ART-879

PICK UP YOUR EARS, HENRY

by PATRICIA BRENNAN DEMUTH
illustrated by BOB BARNER

MACMILLAN PUBLISHING COMPANY
New York
Maxwell Macmillan Canada
Toronto
Maxwell Macmillan International
New York   Oxford   Singapore   Sydney

 Macmillan Publishing Company is part of the Maxwell Communication Group of Companies. Macmillan Publishing Company, 866 Third Avenue, New York, NY 10022. Maxwell Macmillan Canada, Inc., 1200 Eglinton Avenue East, Suite 200, Don Mills, Ontario M3C 3N1. First edition. Printed in the United States of America. The text of this book is set in 30 pt. Helvetica Bold. The illustrations are rendered in cut paper collage.

1 3 5 7 9 10 8 6 4 2

Library of Congress Cataloging-in-Publication Data. Demuth, Patricia. Pick up your ears, Henry / by Patricia Brennan Demuth ; illustrated by Bob Barner. — 1st ed. p. cm. Summary: A puppy hears many sounds as he searches through the barnyard for his mother. ISBN 0-02-728465-4 [1. Dogs—Fiction. 2. Farm life—Fiction. 3. Sound—Fiction.] I. Barner, Bob, ill. II. Title.

PZ7.D4122Pi 1992 [E]—dc20 91-27162

For my sister, Mary—P. B.D.

For my parents—B.B.

"Where's Mom?"

"Pick up your ears, Henry."

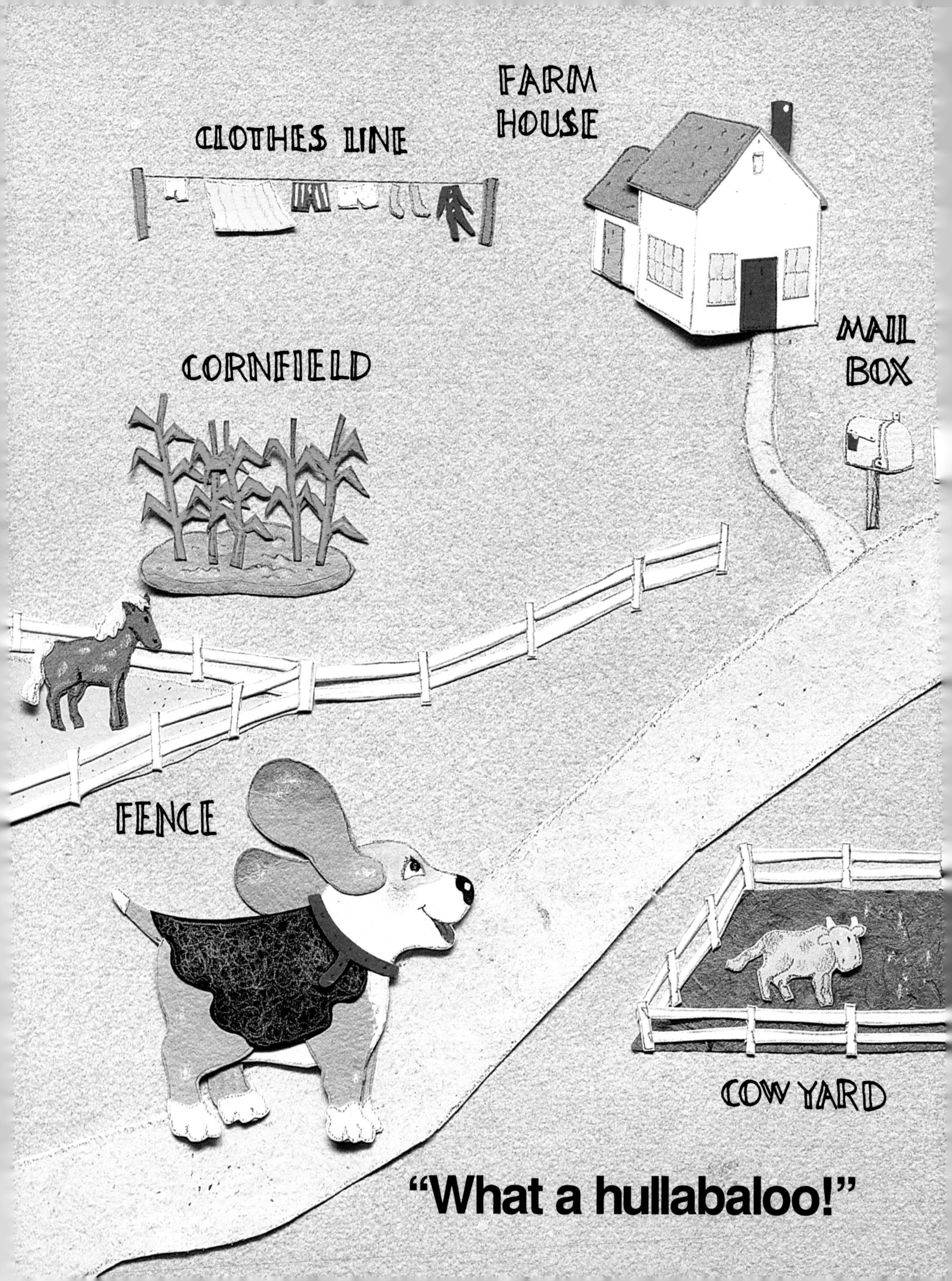

"What a hullabaloo!"

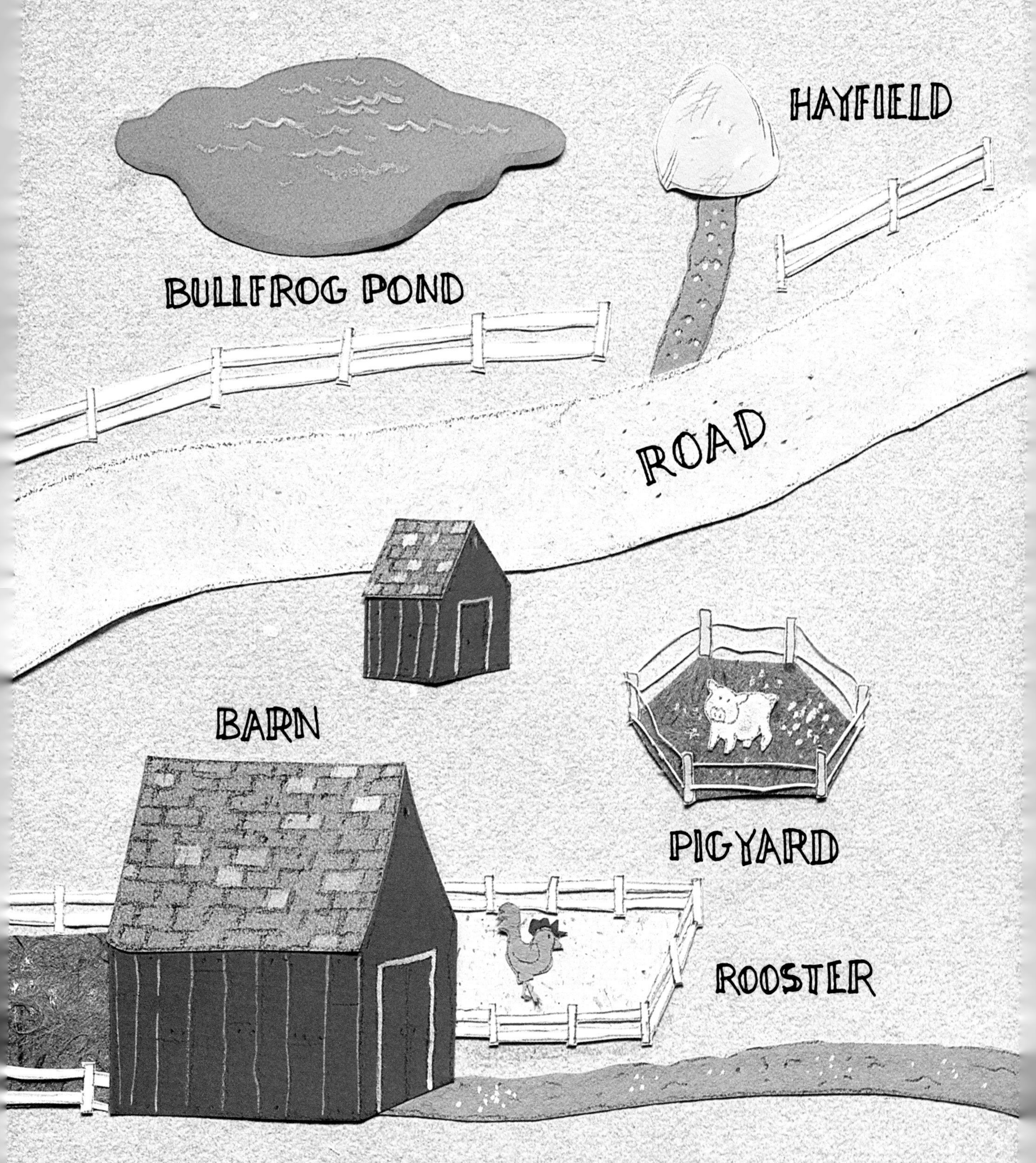

Bang-bang-bang.

BANG!

The farmer is pounding nails.

Swish-sh-sh-sh-sh.
Swoosh-sh-sh-sh-sh.

Leaves in the cornfield blow.

Ribbit. Ribbit.

Grunty little bullfrogs.

Cht, ffffffffff.
Cht, ffffffffff.

The farmer's son shovels corn.

Cre-e-e-ea-k.

Wham!

Cre-e-e-ea-k!

Wind blows the old barn door.

Thump. Thump-thump.

The cows' tails swat flies and more flies.

Rrrrr-eeeee!

A cricket chirping high and sweet.

Flup. Fluppity, flup-flup.

Wet sheets on the clotheslines.

Bawk! Bk-bk-bk-bk-bk-bk, bawk!

Bossy rooster.

Oo-wee, oo-wee, ooo-WEEEEEE!

Pigs, always hungry.

Crunch. Scrunch.

Tractor tires on gravel.

Z-Z-Z-Z-Z-Z-Z

"Someone's snoring!"

“Mom!”

Hmmm...